The Little Red Hen

A Tale about Cooperation

Retold by Justine A. Ciovacco
Illustrated by Loretta Lustig

D1370201

Famous Fables™

Reader's Digest Young Families

The Little Red Hen lived in a cozy little home of her own on Farmer Ferguson's farm. Her home was very tidy and filled with things she made herself—cups and bowls made from nutshells, tablecloths from leathery oak leaves, and rugs woven from dried grasses. And there were lots of flowers all around.

All the other farm animals knew the Little Red Hen worked hard to keep her home so nice.

The Little Red Hen had three good friends—the Cat, the Dog, and the Pig. When the Little Red Hen wasn't busy, she liked nothing better than to visit with them. Unlike the Little Red Hen, though, the Cat, the Dog, and the Pig spent most of their time talking, sleeping, or just lying around, waiting for Farmer Ferguson to feed them.

One day the Little Red Hen took a walk to search for food. She poked around as she walked, dipping her beak into the grassy patches on Farmer Ferguson's farm.

"Hmm, nothing," she said worriedly. Then she pecked a bit of something different. It was kernels of wheat.

"Grain!" cried the Little Red Hen. She knew she shouldn't eat the tiny, hard grains. She would plant them instead and help them grow. Then she'd have a field of wheat to make into flour to bake fresh bread.

The Little Red Hen hurried to her friends the Cat, the Dog, and the Pig, who were chatting beneath a shady tree.

"Look what I've found!" said the Little Red Hen. "Grains of wheat!"

"Yum, let's eat them," said the Pig. "It's a small meal, but it will do."

"No, no," said the Little Red Hen. "Who wants to help me plant these grains of wheat?"

"Not I," said the Cat, playing with a ball of yarn.

"Not I," said the Dog, swatting a fly away with his tail.

"Not I," said the Pig with a bored-sounding snort.

"Then I will do it myself," said the Little Red Hen. And she did.

The Little Red Hen planted the kernels in a sunny place. She watered the growing plants every day.

Soon the wheat grew tall and golden. It blew gently back and forth in the breeze.

The Little Red Hen was proud of her wheat. But there was more work to be done. She hurried over to her friends, who were resting by a pond.

"The wheat is tall and golden," said the Little Red Hen. "Who will help me cut it down?"

"Not I," said the Cat, licking her paw clean.

"Not I," said the Dog, resting his chin on the ground.

"Not I," said the Pig, sniffing the pond water with his big snout.

"Then I will do it myself," said the Little Red Hen. And she did.

The Little Red Hen used her sharp beak to separate the edible kernels from the stalks. But she was the only one doing this. So she hurried over to the Cat, the Dog, and the Pig, who were lying out in the sun, to ask for help.

"The kernels must be separated from the stalks," she said. "Who will help me?"

"Not I," said the Cat, turning over on her left side.

"Not I," said the Dog, resting on his paws.

"Not I," said the Pig as he waddled back to his pen filled with cool mud.

"Then I will do it myself," said the Little Red Hen. And she did.

Now the wheat was ready to be taken to the mill. There, it could be ground into flour.

The Little Red Hen swept the kernels of wheat into a sack with her wing. The sack was very heavy. So the Little Red Hen went to find her friends. They were eating a small midday meal that Farmer Ferguson had left out for them.

"The wheat is ready to be ground into flour," said the Little Red Hen. "Who will to help me carry it to the mill?"

"Not I," said the Cat, licking her whiskers.

"Not I," said the Dog, his mouth still full.

"Not I," said the Pig, sticking his snout back into his food.

"Then I will do it myself," said the Little Red Hen. And she did.

It was hard work, but the Little Red Hen carried the sack of wheat to the mill all by herself. She returned to the farm with a bag of flour a few hours later. Finally, she could make her bread! She hurried over to her friends to share the news. They were snoozing under a shady tree.

"I've got the flour!" the Little Red Hen told them.

"Who will help me make the bread?"

"Not I," said the Cat as she yawned.

"Not I," said the Dog as he opened and closed one eye.

"Not I," said the Pig before he went back to snoring.

"Then I will do it myself," said the Little Red Hen. And she did.

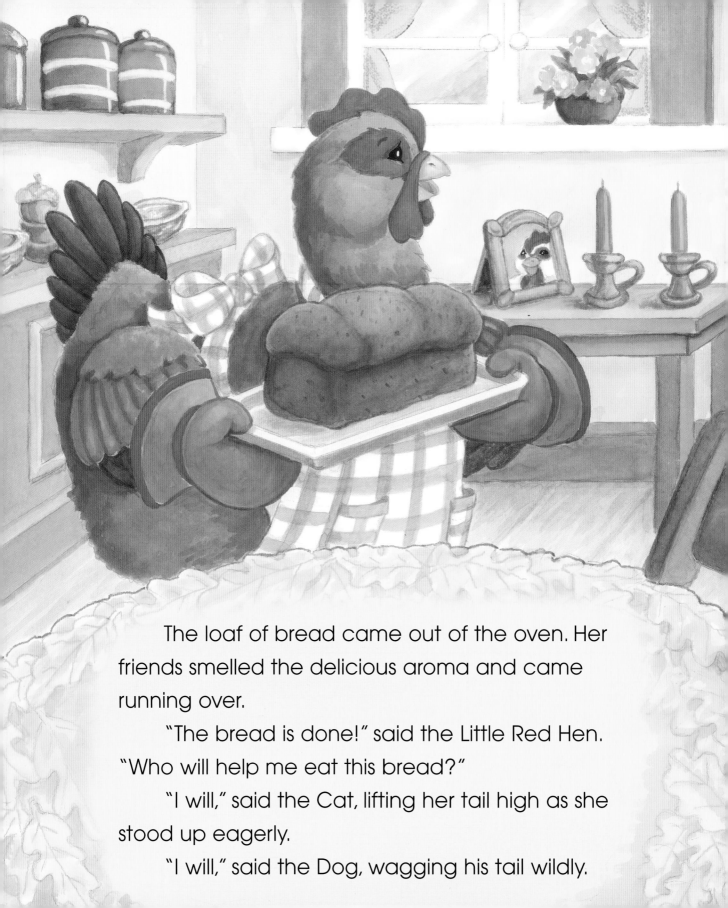

The loaf of bread came out of the oven. Her friends smelled the delicious aroma and came running over.

"The bread is done!" said the Little Red Hen. "Who will help me eat this bread?"

"I will," said the Cat, lifting her tail high as she stood up eagerly.

"I will," said the Dog, wagging his tail wildly.

"I will," said the Pig, grunting happily.

But the Little Red Hen said to them, "Anyone who helped me plant the grain, harvest the wheat, carry the wheat to the mill, or bake the loaf can share this bread with me."

The others looked down at their feet.

"Then I guess I'll do this myself, too." And she did.

Famous Fables, Lasting Virtues Tips for Parents

Now that you've read The Little Red Hen, *use these pages as a guide to teach your child the virtues in the story. By talking about the story and its message and engaging in the suggested activities, you can help your child develop good judgment and a strong moral character.*

About Cooperation

Children learn about cooperation by observing family members, through their own trial-and-error experiences, and through imaginative play. If you and other family members cooperate, your child will learn how much easier and faster it is to get work done when everyone helps. The rewards of cooperating are many—a sense of accomplishment, a boost to self-esteem, more time for play.

1. *Talk with your child about your own experiences.* Children enjoy hearing stories about people they know. Share examples from your own life to show your child how adults cooperate in order to get work done and compromise when there is a difference of opinion. Simple examples, such as family chores or which movie to see, are understood by even the youngest children.

2. *Teamwork.* Explain that cooperating works best when people think of themselves as members of a team, working together for a common goal. Every team member's ideas and feelings matter, but this doesn't necessarily mean the job gets done in a way that pleases everyone.

3. *Work together.* Children may get upset when it is time to clean up or do other chores. If you offer to help, especially to get the task started, you may find your child willing to follow your lead.

4. *Turn work into a game.* Whenever possible, make chores fun. If clothes need to be put into a hamper or washer, for example, pretend you are playing a basketball game and gently toss the clothes into the "hoop." Give points and a small reward to the winner.